HE CHANGED OUR GREAT NATION

ABRAHAM LINCOLN

By DONALD L. SCHUCK

Illustrated by MARCIN PIWOWARSKI

MANKATO, MINNESOTA

Published by Cantata Learning
1710 Roe Crest Drive
North Mankato, MN 56003
www.cantatalearning.com

Library of Congress Control Number: 2014938273
978-1-63290-088-3 (hardcover/CD)
978-1-63290-167-5 (paperback/CD)
978-1-63290-402-7 (paperback)

He Changed our Great Nation: Abraham Lincoln by Donald L. Schuck
Illustrated by Marcin Piwowarski

Book design by Tim Palin Creative
Music produced by Wes Schuck
Audio recorded, mixed, and mastered at Two Fish Studios, Mankato, MN

Printed in the United States of America.

Abraham Lincoln
(1809-1865)

Abraham Lincoln was the 16th president of the United States of America. He led the country during the **Civil War.** President Lincoln believed everyone should live freely, including **slaves**.

Born in Kentucky, in the year 1809,

a boy named Abe Lincoln helped
this country shine.

He changed the way we treated
people just like you and me.

He was the 16th person to accept the **presidency**.

Abe never thought his looks were the best on **Capitol Hill**. Now his face is on the penny and on the five-dollar bill. You see, his confidence in what was right gave him the courage to free the slaves and change the **laws**, once and for all.

President Lincoln introduced the **Emancipation Proclamation**.
He found that ending slavery was a difficult situation.
The North and South had their opinions. They couldn't seem to agree.
Abe knew what was right and that all people should be free.

It was a time for exploration, and the United States was growing strong.

But becoming larger meant more power and trouble getting along.

Different opinions lead to arguments and sometimes people fight.

It's difficult to get along when both sides think they're right.

The United States split up
and became the North and South.

Some states wanted different things
than the whole country would allow.

The country was at Civil War
and many disagreed.

But Abe knew what was right
and that all people should be free.

President Lincoln introduced the Emancipation Proclamation.
He found that ending slavery was a difficult situation.
The North and South had their opinions. They couldn't seem to agree.
Abe knew what was right and that all people should be free.

Freedom has been given to us by those who came before.
We can learn from our history. This we can't ignore!
Abe Lincoln was a leader. And you can be one, too.
Just do what you know is right and work hard in school.

President Lincoln introduced the Emancipation Proclamation.
He found that ending slavery was a difficult situation.
The North and South had their opinions. They couldn't seem to agree.
Abe knew what was right and that all people should be free.

GLOSSARY

Capitol Hill—the neighborhood in Washington D.C. where many American government leaders live and work

Civil War—(1861-1865) the battle between states in the North and South that led to the end of slavery in the United States

Emancipation Proclamation—an important government paper that helped free slaves

law—a rule made by the government that must be obeyed

presidency—the term during which a president holds office

slave—a person who is owned by another person

He Changed Our Great Nation: Abraham Lincoln

Donald L. Schuck

Country

ACTIVITY QUESTIONS

1. Abe Lincoln was a very good problem solver. If you were a leader how would you help others solve a problem?
2. What traits does a leader need to have to be a good problem solver?

TO LEARN MORE

Edison, Erin. *Abraham Lincoln*. Mankato, Minn.: Capstone Press, 2013.

Kalman, Maira. *Looking at Lincoln*. New York: Nancy Paulsen, 2012.

Mayer, Cassie. *Abraham Lincoln*. Mankato, Minn.: Capstone Press, 2008.

Meltzer, Brad. *I Am Abraham Lincoln*. New York, NY: Dial, 2014.